THE LAST REVERIE

ISHAAN

BLUEROSE PUBLISHERS
India | U.K.

Copyright © Ishaan 2024

All rights reserved by author. No part of this publication may be reproduced, stored in a retrieval system or transmitted in any form or by any means, electronic, mechanical, photocopying, recording or otherwise, without the prior permission of the author. Although every precaution has been taken to verify the accuracy of the information contained herein, the publisher assumes no responsibility for any errors or omissions. No liability is assumed for damages that may result from the use of information contained within.

BlueRose Publishers takes no responsibility for any damages, losses, or liabilities that may arise from the use or misuse of the information, products, or services provided in this publication.

For permissions requests or inquiries regarding this publication, please contact:

BLUEROSE PUBLISHERS
www.BlueRoseONE.com
info@bluerosepublishers.com
+91 8882 898 898
+4407342408967

Cover Designed by Germancreative

ISBN: 978-93-6783-246-2

First Edition: December 2024

DEDICATION

For my friends Sayantan (Baba) and Rahul (RKT),
whose trust and faith in my writing ignited my spark

ABOUT THE AUTHOR

Ishaan is the pen name of Arka Prava Nayek, a writer based in Bengaluru, India. He was born in Memari, a small town in West Bengal and spent most of his childhood in hostels at Ramakrishna Mission Vidyalaya, Narendrapur. After graduating from National Institute of Technology, Durgapur, he is currently working in data analytics in one of the Big 4 consulting firms. His passion for storytelling, combined with his background in science and tech, inspired him to write science fiction stories.

He was shortlisted for Satyajit Ray Film and Television Institute's Direction and Screenwriting in 2019. His team's sci-fi thriller project The Metaverse Connection was selected to be showcased at AVGC panel at Cannes Film Festival 2023.

To learn more about the writer and his projects, follow him on
Instagram: @ishaanwrites7
Facebook: https://www.facebook.com/ishaanwrites7

ACKNOWLEDGMENTS

I am eternally grateful to my parents, Amitava and Mukul, for their unwavering support throughout this journey. My heartfelt thanks to my sister, Chandra, for her insightful feedback on the story and the amazing cover design idea. I owe a debt of gratitude to my dear friends, Sayantan (Baba) and Rahul (RKT), for their boundless encouragement and belief in me, even when I doubted myself. I am also thankful to my friend and collaborator, Abhishek Maji, for his invaluable advice and guidance. I would like to express my thanks to my cousin, Some, for his helpful suggestions. Finally, I am extremely indebted to all my beta readers for their constructive criticism and feedback on this project.

CHAPTER ONE

It was a day unlike any other. The air crackled with a tension Doc could almost taste. He knew that today might change everything, and the uncertainty made his breath catch in his throat. A cold knot of dread twisted in his gut.

Doc steered Eve through the worn wooden door of Old Oak Tavern, holding the door open for her, the rustic bell chiming overhead as they entered. The pub, nestled on a quiet street corner, had changed little over the years, its walls still adorned with antique tools and faded sepia photographs of the town's earlier days. A surge of nostalgia swept him; it was like stepping back in time.

The air hung thick with the aroma of roasted meats, spilled ale and aged wood. Under the warm glow of antique brass chandeliers, laughter echoed off the wooden beams of the pub and erupted in symphony with the clinking of tankards and the rhythmic stomping of dancing feet. Oak tables, scarred with countless nights of revelry, groaned under the weight of frothing tankards and overflowing platters. A band tucked away in the corner strummed out a soft rock ballad, their mellow tune weaving its way through the happy chaos.

A jovial group of locals, their cheeks flushed with warmth and merriment, swayed in a circle to the gentle strum of acoustic guitars and steady beat of hand drums. Groups of friends huddled around tables, sharing stories and jokes, their chatter vibrating off the aged wood paneling and dancing between the rafters. Couples nestled in the tables, their whispers inaudible over the soft melody that filled the dimly lit space. A crackling fire roared in the hearth and candlelight flickered in the tables, casting long dancing shadows on the walls adorned with vintage brewery advertisements and dusty portraits. The weathered oak bar, its surface gleaming under the glow of antique lamps, was a bustling hub of activity, with the barkeep deftly juggling orders and engaging in friendly banter with the patrons. The pub, a cozy relic from another era, was alive.

Guiding Eve to their old table, tucked away in a corner of the pub, Doc's fingers brushed against the coarse grain of the wood, his mind racing through the countless stories shared here. He pulled out a chair for Eve, the same one she had used on that pivotal night years ago, his heart tight with hope and fear.

With a smile that didn't quite reach his eyes, Doc

waved over the server, a new face in an old setting. "Could we have two Shepherd's pies and Caesar salads, please? And two pints of the house beer," he ordered, the words carrying a meaning heavier than mere dinner choices. Each item was a deliberate echo of the past, a script he hoped would stir some ember of memory in Eve.

As the server nodded and disappeared back to the kitchen, Doc turned his attention to Eve. She sat serene and composed, her eyes observing the pub with a detached curiosity that clawed at his heart. He watched her closely, searching for any sign of recognition, any hint of the emotions they'd shared during their first visit here. But her face was as unreadable as ever, her expression unyielding.

The meals arrived, steaming and fragrant, placed before them along with a clink of cutlery. Doc gestured at Eve with an enthusiastic smile. "How does it feel?" he prompted, his voice threading through the growing din of the pub.

Eve looked around quickly, then up at him. "It's great, I like the ambience." she commented politely, her tone neutral, clinical even. A ghost of a smile touched her lips, then vanished, leaving only a carefully composed mask in its wake. No trace of recollection, no spark of the past that Doc so desperately wanted to see.

They ate mostly in silence, Doc's cheerfulness crumbling with each bite. He had hoped that the familiar setting, the shared meal, and the ambient strains of a soft rock ballad from the jukebox might rekindle something within Eve, some flicker of who she was meant to be. But as the meal progressed, it became painfully clear that no combination of sensory cues could bridge the gap that his ambitions had created.

Doc pushed the plate away, his appetite lost to disappointment. He watched Eve as she neatly placed her cutlery on the empty plate, her movements precise, devoid of the warmth and spontaneity that he was hoping to see in her. It was in this moment, amid the low hum of conversations and the occasional clink of glasses, that Doc felt the full weight of what was lost.

The pub around him felt smaller suddenly, the walls inching closer as the reality of his situation set in. He had succeeded in recreating Eve, but in doing so, had he lost her forever? The question hung heavily in the air, unanswered, as the server cleared their table and the last notes of the song played out.

Doc stared deep inside Eve's eyes, something about her eyes - a depthlessness, like gazing into an abyss. They reflected the overhead lights, but no spark of life seemed to dance behind them.

The night was young, but the atmosphere inside Old Oak Tavern was timeless, suspended between the nostalgic tunes from the old jukebox and the soft, dim lighting that gave the ambience a romantic touch. Doc found himself in the midst of a predetermined setting, struggling with a sense of déjà vu.

He led Eve toward the jukebox that stood in the

corner of the pub, its surface a mosaic of fingerprints and faded song titles. He scrolled through the selections with a sense of purpose, stopping at a folk rock band they had listened to years ago. With a press of a button, the machine whirred to life, filling the pub with the familiar tune of acoustic guitars and the gravelly texture of rustic vocals. Doc's eyes briefly closed as he let the music transport him back to a time when everything seemed simpler, when he had all that he wanted in the world and life was perfect.

Opening his eyes, he turned to Eve, searching her features for any sign of remembrance, any glimmer of the emotions that the music might stir within her. Her face, ever serene and beautiful, showed no change, her eyes reflecting the dancing lights of the pub with a clarity that was both miraculous and heartbreaking.

Not one to give up easily, Doc decided to push further, to recreate yet another piece of their past. He approached Eve with a hesitant smile and offered his hand. "Would you like to join me for a dance?" he asked, his voice soft and hopeful.

Eve nodded, her response automatic, and allowed him to lead her to the small dance floor near the bandstand. As they moved together to the rhythm of the music, Doc's movements were filled with a hesitant longing. He tried to lead as he had once, years ago, when every step wasn't just a dance move but an intimate moment filled with laughter and shared secrets. Now, Eve followed his lead with precision and grace, her steps perfectly timed but mechanical, lacking the spontaneity.

Doc's heart ached with the realization that the Eve he had hoped for - the one who would laugh and dance and evoke emotions with genuine warmth - was perhaps forever beyond his reach. The song played on, a haunting melody that now seemed more a requiem for love lost than a backdrop to a romantic scene.

As the last chords of the song faded into the murmur of the pub, Doc felt a pang of defeat sharper than any he had felt in any of his numerous scientific endeavors. He stopped dancing abruptly, his hand slipping away from Eve's. He looked at her, really looked, hoping to see even a spark of what had been. But her face, though beautiful, was as impassive as ever.

"I'm sorry, I have to go," Doc muttered, more to himself than to Eve. His voice was strained, carrying the weight of his disappointment. "Umm… Early day tomorrow."

In that moment, both creator and creation stood alone, separated by the very advancements that were meant to bring them closer, each isolated by their own unique confines of existence.

Without waiting for her response, he turned and headed for the exit. Eve remained on the dance floor, perplexed. Her expression was unreadable, her gaze fixed on the now silent jukebox, a symbol of Doc's failed attempt to reach through the veil of technology into the remnants of her human past. His footsteps echoed in the dimly lit pub, each footfall a thud of disappointment. He pushed through the heavy wooden door. The cool night air hit his face as he stepped outside, the sudden change in temperature mirroring the cold realization that had settled over his heart. As he walked away, the sounds of the pub faded into the background, swallowed by the night.

"Eli, wait!" Eve's voice, sharp and desperate, cut through the night. Doc didn't stop, didn't turn, the gravel crunching under his boots. A wave of disappointment washed over him. This wasn't the Eve he was expecting. This was a stranger lost in a labyrinth.

His car, waiting silently in the shadows, beckoned him. His fingers tightened around the car keys. A wave of nausea washed over him, the same feeling he got every time he let himself hope, only for it to be crushed. He slid inside, the leather seats cool against his skin. The engine came to life as he hit the ignition, a low growl that echoed his own frustration. He rested his forehead on the steering wheel, his breath coming in ragged gasps. The world blurred into a dance of shadows. He could hear her muffled sobs through the window, her pleas growing more desperate with each passing second.

"Eli, please!" Eve's hand tapped against the window. He squeezed his eyes shut, the sound of her voice a painful reminder of their fractured bond.

"Please, just listen to me," Eve begged.

"I've heard it all before," Doc said, his voice cold and flat.

He gritted his teeth, the anger bubbling up inside

him threatening to spill over. Doc gripped the steering wheel, his knuckles white, He had to get out of here, away from the echoes of what they once were. With a heavy heart, he slammed the accelerator. The car roared to life, tires squealing as it shot forward and sped away, leaving Eve standing alone in the rain, her cries fading into the distance.

He glanced at the rearview mirror as a teardrop trickled down his eye, catching a glimpse of Eve shrinking into the distance. A pang of guilt stabbed at his heart, but he pushed it down. He couldn't let her pull him back into the chaos, after she shattered his trust. Eve and the pub slowly blurred out of focus in the rearview mirror. The car's tires squealed as he turned a corner, the world tilting on its axis.

There is no other way, Doc thought. He had to take that final leap that he had hoped he wouldn't have to do. The hardest part of ending something is starting all over again.

Doc focused on the road ahead, the city lights his only guide. He was leaving Eve behind, but he knew the shadows of their past would always linger. The journey was just beginning, and the path ahead was uncertain. But one thing was clear, there was no turning back. He didn't look back.

With one hand on the steering wheel, he reached out into his pocket with the other hand and pulled out a jade necklace. He held it up to the light, the jade stone shimmering like a teardrop. He closed his eyes for an instant, the memories flooding back. Her laughter, her smile, her touch...

He opened his eyes, a single tear tracing a path down his cheek. He clutched the necklace tightly, a lifeline to a past that was slipping away.

"I'll remember you, Helen," he whispered. "I promise."

CHAPTER TWO

The entrance to Doc's underground lab lay hidden in an abandoned tunnel, swallowed by the shadows of the city's forgotten outskirts.

Doc took a deep breath, the stale air of the tunnel doing little to prepare him for what lay ahead. His footsteps echoed through the tunnel's cavernous space as he walked, finally reaching the ladder that ascended to the maintenance hatch in his lab. The rusted ladder creaked under his weight, each rung a protest against time and abandonment. He pulled open the hatch and emerged into the entrance of the lab. Dust motes danced in the air, illuminated by the faint glow of sunlight coming in through the cracked windows. The lab was a ghost of its former glory.

The lab was a graveyard of scientific ambition. Abandoned projects lay scattered, half-finished prototypes gathering dust. Doc ran a hand along a workbench, the cold metal a stark reminder of his past life. He needed to restore power to this place to kickstart his operation. The low roar of the backup generator filled the silence as he powered it up, the lights flickering to life.

The biometric scanner glowed expectantly. Doc felt a faint glimmer of hope. But he hesitated, his eyes scanning the lab for any sign of unwanted surveillance. He placed his hand on the scanner, the cool surface registering his unique print. A green light flashed, followed by the whirring of a long-dormant system.

A shrill alarm shattered the silence. Doc cursed, his heart pounding in his chest. Red lights strobed, casting long shadows that danced menacingly on the walls. He knew he had very limited time before security arrived.

Doc sprinted to the main console, his fingers flying across the controls. The alarm continued its relentless screeching, a siren song of impending doom. He punched in a series of commands, bypassing the security protocols.

The lab's main doors slid open, revealing a darkened corridor. Doc didn't hesitate. He slipped through the opening, the alarm's wail fading as the doors slammed shut behind him. He was back in the game, the adrenaline coursing through his veins.

He hurried through the corridor till he reached his lab room. Inside, the space was a catacomb of the past, strewn with relics of a once-glistening career. Tarnished trophies and certificates clung to the walls like remnants of a shipwreck to the ocean floor. Amidst this graveyard of his former glories, Doc went over to his computer terminal at the center of the lab and bent over it, the intense focus etching lines deeper into his weathered face.

The bulb overhead flickered, casting erratic shadows across the desk cluttered with disused gadgets and faded photographs of peers who had long since disavowed him. A sudden loud beep broke the monotony. The screen lit up with an alert message. Doc's face turned pale. The message on the bold red font read: 'Warning! Intruder detected'.

Doc's gaze remained locked on the computer terminal, his hands steady, betraying none of the turmoil that notification might herald. It kept beeping again and again, pulling him from the terminal screen back into the urgency of the situation.

Doc's heart thudded against his ribs, a primal response from a body too worn for the kind of escape the message implied. He couldn't let it go when he was so close to what he sought. He was fully aware of the dangers of the mission when he decided to partake in it. His breath caught in his chest as he read the three words again and again, each one a nail in the coffin of his current situation. They knew. They had found him here.

"Doc, I advise immediate evacuation. Your heart rate has elevated dangerously," chimed the voice of his digital assistant, a sophisticated program he had developed in better days to assist him with all matters of the lab. Her concern was clinical, devoid of warmth, yet it spurred him into action. He couldn't go back the way he came in. That would be too risky.

"Yes, activate the escape protocol," he commanded, his voice mingling with fear and determination.

"As you wish, Doc." The digital assistant's voice was calm, a stark contrast to Doc's mounting panic.

Doc turned to a section of the lab wall that looked no different from the rest. He pressed hard against a seemingly random pattern of faded wallpaper, and a panel slid open with a hiss of releasing air, revealing a dark, narrow crawl space.

In the fleeting moments of decision, Doc's hands were steady as he reached into the false bottom drawer of his workstation. Amidst the chaos of his impending escape, this singular action was performed with surgical precision. The hard drive - compact, unassuming, yet holding the entirety of his life's most critical work - slid soundlessly into his palm. Years of research on Eve, the android project that was both his life's work and his potential redemption, rested heavily in his grip. He tucked it into the inner pocket of his worn jacket.

His preparations for this moment were meticulous, born of paranoia and foresight. It was an escape route that he had mapped out during his early days in this hideout. He grabbed a backpack prepacked with essentials - water, non-perishable food, a basic first-aid kit and a flashlight.

With one last glance at the lab, his former sanctuary, Doc squeezed into the narrow opening in front of him. The wall panel closed silently behind him, sealing off the world he knew, perhaps forever. Each step was a move away from his past - a past littered with ambition and ultimately, betrayal. The path ahead was pitch-black and the walls seemed to close in on him. He turned on the flashlight and gripped it with his teeth. He inched forward, his heart hammering against his ribs. The space grew tighter, forcing him to move his body into uncomfortable positions. Panic clawed at his throat as the space narrowed to a suffocating squeeze. He gasped for air, his limbs screaming in protest. But the thought of turning back was even more terrifying. With a desperate surge of adrenaline, he pushed through the final constriction and emerged into a slightly larger space. Relief washed over him as he caught sight of the hatch.

Doc's breath hitched as he wrestled with the rusted hatch, its hinges protesting with a shriek that echoed through the deserted space and pierced the blaring alarm. Sweat stung his eyes, blurring his vision, but he couldn't stop. He yanked again, the metal groaning in surrender, and a blast of cold air rushed out, carrying the scent of damp earth. The hatch creaked open, revealing a gaping hole of darkness - the entrance to the tunnels, a vein running to the heart of the city's underbelly. He hesitated, the abyss beckoning and repelling him at once. Then, he lowered himself into the void.

As he moved deeper into the shadows, Doc allowed himself a brief look back - not in sentiment, but in strategic consideration of what he was leaving unprotected. Then, squaring his shoulders against the damp chill of the tunnel, Doc disappeared into the bowels of the city, driven by the primal need to survive and the burning hope to rebuild.

The tunnel loomed before him, a dark maw ready to swallow him into the city's underbelly. Doc switched on his flashlight, the beam slicing through the oppressive darkness. As Doc ran through the tunnels, the sound of his boots on the damp concrete echoed back at him like a metronome of urgency. The walls, slick with condensation and the residues of neglect, felt close enough to constrict. But Doc's focus was laser-sharp; his path forward was etched in his memory, a route rehearsed countless times in anticipation of this exact moment.

The air grew heavier as he delved deeper, the stench of the sewers mingling with the metallic taste of fear in his mouth. Here, beneath the surface, the city's pulse was a distant rumble, its chaos muted by layers of earth and stone. Doc moved with an efficiency born of desperation, the beam of his flashlight darting ahead, a silent sentinel clearing the shadows from his path.

The tunnel seemed endless and Doc's panic grew worse with each passing moment. Time became a malleable concept, stretching taut in the cramped tunnel. Eventually, the passage began to ascend, signaling his approach to the exit. Doc could catch a glimpse of the light at the end of the tunnel. Doc's muscles tensed, preparing to breach the surface. He paused at the base of the ladder leading up to the manhole cover, listening for any signs of the world above. Silence greeted him - not comforting, but a void waiting to be filled with unknown consequences.

With a push that taxed his limbs, Doc dislodged the manhole cover, the grating sound piercing loud in the stillness of the night. He emerged cautiously, his head swiveling as his eyes adjusted to the dim light provided by the distant street lamps. The area was secluded, an abandoned section of the city that few had reason to visit, shrouded in shadows and dereliction. His escape route had led him well, a strategic point meticulously chosen for its obscurity.

Pulling himself fully out of the sewer, Doc replaced the cover with care, masking his exit back into the world. He paused to catch his breath, the cool air sharp in his lungs. It was then that he turned to gaze upon the distant chaos, his former lab now the epicenter of an orchestrated storm.

From his vantage point, the scene unfolded with the surreal quality of a nightmare. Blue and red lights painted the night, a chaotic ballet of emergency vehicles swarming the place he had once called his sanctuary. Even from miles away, the flurry of activity was palpable, the urgency of the raid transmitted through the beaming lights and distant clamor.

Doc felt a pang of loss so acute it bordered on physical pain. That lab had been more than just a collection of equipments and data; it had been his last connection to a past life, to a time when his ambitions had promised to elevate humanity, not drive him into the shadows. Relief mingled with this sorrow, bittersweet and heavy. Relief that he had escaped, that his work on Eve was secure for now - but at what cost?

His chest heaved with a deep, weary sigh. Turning away from the chaos, Doc set his sights on the darkened skyline ahead, the city a labyrinth of lights and shadows. Somewhere out there lay his next step, a path forward shrouded in uncertainty but necessary all the same. With a resolve forged in the fires of his trials, he started walking.

CHAPTER THREE

In the shadowed veins of the city, Doc moved stealthily with a hunter's grace, ensuring his presence melted into the dark silence of the night. His new identity, forged not from digital footprints but from necessity, clung to him like a second skin. The hood on his jacket was pulled low over his forehead, a cap shadowing his eyes, while the collar brushed against his stubbled cheeks. Pausing momentarily by a shattered window, he checked his reflection, adjusting the fabric to obscure any features that might betray him.

The back alleys of the city, with their dimly lit alleys and oppressive silences, became his pathways. Doc's eyes now scanned the murky darkness for signs of life. Each shadow could be a sanctuary or threat, each distant footstep a herald of friend or foe. He stopped at the mouth of an alley, his breath a mist in the cold air as he surveyed the street beyond. Seeing it empty, he darted across, his movements a quick dash that carried him into the shadows on the opposite side.

Doc burst onto the rain-slicked streets, his breath forming clouds in the cold night air. The city was a labyrinth of shadows, the neon signs casting an eerie glow on the wet pavement. He pressed himself against a building, his eyes scanning the deserted alleyways. He started moving cautiously, his eyes scanning the shadows for any sign of pursuit. The streets showed no signs of life. He kept moving.

It was on one such street, far removed from the city's pulsating heart, that Doc encountered a relic of society forgotten by progress. A homeless man lay huddled under a tattered blanket below a flickering streetlight, his cart of possessions a barricade against the world. As Doc approached, the man's eyes flicked upward, peering out from beneath his makeshift shelter. They locked eyes for a heartbeat, the man's gaze sharp, then dulled by resignation. Recognizing nothing threatening or useful in the hooded figure before him, he grunted and turned his head away, dismissing Doc back into anonymity.

Doc kept moving with slow, unhurried steps to avoid suspicion, without paying any attention to the lone figure, but that man's eyes followed Doc. A few moments later, the man emerged from the darkness. He clutched a cardboard sign in his grimy hands, the words "THE END IS NIGH" scrawled in crude lettering. Doc stopped a few feet from the man, his gaze drawn to the sign.

"You," the man rasped, his voice rough from disuse.

"You're the one they're looking for."

Doc tensed, instinctively taking a couple of steps back. "Who's looking?" he asked, his voice low.

The man chuckled, a hollow sound that echoed in the empty street. "They're everywhere," he said, his eyes darting nervously. "They see everything."

Doc stepped closer, his boots splashing in a puddle. "Tell me what you know," he demanded, his voice barely a whisper.

The man leaned forward, his breath hot against Doc's face. "They're coming," he hissed. "They're coming for us all."

Suddenly the old man's expression changed, as if some demon had been exorcized from him.

"Spare some change, mister?" the man rasped, his voice rough and gravelly.

Doc stared at him, a flicker of recognition in the man's eyes. "Have I seen you somewhere before?"

The man chuckled, a hollow sound that echoed in the empty street. "We've all seen each other before, in another life, perhaps."

Doc's mind raced. The man's eyes held a strange intensity, a glint of madness that sent a shiver down Doc's spine.

"What's that supposed to mean?" Doc pointed to the cardboard sign, his voice sharp with suspicion.

The man laughed menacingly, it sent a shiver down Doc's spine. "You haven't heard? The world's going to hell. War, famine, pestilence... the whole shebang."

Doc scoffed. "Crazy talk."

"Crazy? Maybe," the man said, his eyes gleaming. "But I'd rather be crazy than dead."

"I have an offer for you." Doc reached into his pocket, withdrawing a few crisp notes. "I need your clothes. And in return, you get this."

The man's eyes widened, greed replacing suspicion. A crooked smile started to form on his face. "You serious?"

"Dead serious." Doc held out the money, the notes fluttering in the breeze.

The man hesitated, then snatched the money, a wicked grin spreading across his face. "You got yourself a deal, mate."

Continuing his trek, Doc remained vigilant, his senses tuned to the dark silence of the night that permeated the city. His caution was justified when a soft whir overhead signaled the presence of a surveillance drone. Instinctively, he ducked behind a nearby dumpster, holding his breath as the mechanical sentinel hovered. Its camera scanned the area, a sweeping gaze searching for anomalies in the quiet night. The ominous red light on its head signaled that it was on a 'search and destroy' mission, instructed to kill if the target was detected in sight. Doc remained still, a statue among refuse, until the drone buzzed away, its mission unfulfilled. He exhaled slowly, the danger postponed but not evaded.

The industrial district loomed ahead, a graveyard of the city's once-thriving manufacturing prowess. Here, amid rusting machinery and skeletal frameworks of factories, lay Sam's sanctuary. The gate creaked ominously as Doc pushed it open, the screeching sound cutting through the silence like a wail. He paused, listening for any echo of his intrusion, but the night remained still. With cautious steps, he navigated the cluttered lot, each vehicle and piece of machinery casting grotesque shadows under the moonlight.

Sam's trailer, a decrepit relic itself, sat isolated at the far end of the lot. Its windows were dark, its metal siding pockmarked with rust. As Doc approached, the reality of his situation pressed down upon him. This trailer was a far cry from the sterile environment of his lab, from the world he had once known. It was a reminder of how far he had fallen, of how desperate he had become.

He stood before the trailer door, his hand raised to knock. Hesitation gripped him, the weight of his decisions, of his current reality, anchoring his feet to the ground. This was no mere visit, it was a plea for asylum; to protect his work, his life.

Doc stood in the shadow of the rusting metal door, the coarse chill of the night air biting into his skin. His hand hovered, tentative and unsteady, inches from the cold, pitted surface of Sam's trailer door. A profound hesitation gripped him, a cocktail of dread and faint hope stirring in his chest. Here, on the threshold of refuge or rejection, Doc drew a shuddering breath, each inhalation thick with the weight of desperation.

Finally, he knocked, the hollow sound against the

thin metal seemed to echo down the dark corridors of his past. He desperately hoped for an answer from the other side, each passing second slowly choking the hope that he was harboring in his heart. The door parted open slightly and a pair of eyes peeked at him from inside, stopping the endless wait and jolting Doc back to the present moment. The eyes widened in shock as they settled on Doc. The door swung open completely. A slender man stood there, framed by the dim light spilling from inside the trailer. His features, once familiar, now bore the marks of hard times. His expression revealed suspicion and an undeniable trace of curiosity.

"Eli?" The man was surprised, almost like seeing a ghost. His voice was rough, disbelieving.

"Hey, Sam. How are you holding up, old buddy?" Doc paused, expecting a response from his friend, but none came. "Gonna let me in?" He forced a smile.

The man on the other side opened the door ajar and gasped again, unable to believe his eyes.

"Doc, I can't believe it's you! I thought we were done for good," There was anger and contempt in Sam's voice.

"Let's just sit down and talk, shall we?" Doc said in defense. "It's been a while since we last saw each other. I could barely recognize you."

Sam's brow furrowed, his initial shock giving way to curiosity. He stepped aside, allowing Doc more room. Running a hand through his unkempt hair, Sam let out a deep, weary sigh. "Damn, Eli. You look like hell. Come in, then. Let's talk."

Doc entered the trailer and Sam locked the door behind him. Sam had long curly hair dropping on his shoulders, and a small mustache. He was wearing shorts and a long hippie overcoat. It was a dimly lit place with flashy neon bulbs and the smell of tobacco hung heavy in the air.

Inside, the trailer was a labyrinth of scattered electronic parts. Sam motioned towards a rickety chair, its covering cracked and peeling. As Doc took a seat, Sam perched on the edge of an overburdened table that resembled a makeshift workbench, the surface littered with tools and gadgets of various kinds.

"It's good to see you after so long, Sam," Doc said and smiled.

"The feeling is not mutual," Sam said in a displeased voice.

"Can you give me a glass of water, please? It has been quite a long journey."

"Sure. Just don't make yourself too comfortable," Sam added as he went for the fridge. "You'll be out of here soon."

A few moments passed in awkward silence.

"Eli? What the hell are you doing here?" Sam's voice, gruff with surprise and edged with a barely concealed annoyance, broke the tense silence. He handed a glass of cold water to Doc. He took out a cigarette from his jacket pocket and lit it.

"Sam, I need help," Doc said, his voice low, urgent. "It's about the project. It's about Eve."

With those words, Doc stepped into a new phase of his fight, the stakes now higher than ever. Sam's face hardened with the weight of old regrets and older loyalties.

Doc stepped forward, the urgency of his plight propelling him into action. "Sam, listen, I - I need your help. It's urgent. I have nowhere else to go," he said, his words tumbling out in a hurried whisper. He glanced around nervously, the cramped space cluttered with the detritus of a life slowly caving in on itself.

"I'm being hunted, Sam. They raided our lab tonight. I managed to escape, but it's only a matter of time before they find me again. I need a place to lay low, to continue my work on Eve," Doc said, the gravity of his situation pressing into every word.

Sam's face was a mask of conflicted emotions. "Eli, you know this isn't a good time. Surveillance, drones, they're everywhere. And after your… disappearance, they've been sniffing everywhere, asking questions. It isn't safe here." He gestured towards a small, flickering screen on the corner of the table. The grainy footage showed different angles of the trailer park, the cameras panning back and forth in a ceaseless vigil.

"Please Sam, you have to help me. For old times' sake."

"Look at this," Sam continued, tapping the screen. "I'm barely scraping by without the feds kicking down my door. You bring a whole new level of heat here."

Doc leaned forward, his eyes earnest and pleading. "I know, Sam, and I wouldn't ask if there was anywhere else I could go. You're the only one I trust. The only one who can help me with this. I need your help to integrate the kernel into Eve's core. Please." The last word hung between them, heavy and fraught with tension.

"I have tried every other approach, calculated every other possibility. Every single one of them failed. This is the only approach that could theoretically work."

For a long moment, Sam just stared at him, the old gears of camaraderie and shared dreams grinding against the reality of their circumstances. Finally, he exhaled sharply and nodded. "Alright, damn it. You can stay. But we do this my way. You understand?"

Doc nodded. He felt a faint hope starting to form in his heart.

"Only one condition. After this, we are done. I don't wanna see your face ever again."

Doc sighed. The words stung him hard, but it was not unexpected. "If that is the way you want it, then so be it."

Sam stood, his figure sagging slightly as if the decision had physically added weight to his shoulders. "I put together whatever I could find to make a surveillance system. That should keep us safe for a while. But we need to keep a low profile. We'll need to set up some ground rules. First, no going outside unless absolutely necessary. And I'll need to beef up the security around here. If you're staying, you're not just hiding, you're doing the heavy lifting. No incoming or outgoing network data. No phone calls. Anything they can use to trace back to us."

Doc nodded, a silent agreement sealing their fate. As Sam began outlining a plan, the direness of their situation settled around them like a shroud, the flicker of the monitor casting long shadows across their faces.

The cramped interior of Sam's trailer was cluttered with remnants of a life left behind. Doc eyed the space with a practiced gaze, assessing every square inch for its potential. Beside him, Sam, still wearing an expression of weary resignation, gestured dismissively at the heaps of discarded machinery and electronic carcasses that filled the room.

"We're going to need to clear all this out," Doc said, stepping over a tangled mess of wires. He dropped his heavy backpack onto a cleared patch of the threadbare carpet and began to unpack the contents - basic lab equipment essential for his ongoing work.

Together, they set to the task with a grim determination. They moved old computer monitors, stacks of faded journals, and broken components that Sam had once hoped to resurrect. The debris of failed projects was swept aside, making room for a temporary lab setup. Doc assembled a small table, its surface soon occupied by a computer terminal, a few circuit boards and various other tools and gadgets.

Once the space was organized, Doc retrieved the hard drive containing all the data on Eve, his groundbreaking android project. With careful hands, he connected it to an old laptop, the screen flickering to life under the strain of booting up. His jaw clenched as he navigated through folders, the silence punctuated only by the soft clicking of the keyboard. Finally, with a visible exhale of relief, his posture relaxed as the files loaded up intact - Eve's data was safe.

Sam, who had been watching the proceedings with a mix of curiosity and skepticism, pushed off from where he leaned against the wall. He ambled over, peering over Doc's shoulder at the lines of code scrolling down the screen.

"All this for what, Eli? You really think you can just pick up where you left off?" Sam's voice was tinged with a cynicism born of experience, his eyes not leaving the screen. "Messing around with artificial intelligence... It's playing with fire. And you know the government's stance on your... experiments."

Doc turned to face him, his eyes meeting Sam's with a fierce resolve. "This isn't just about continuing my research, Sam. It's about completing a vision. Eve could redefine human interaction, revolutionize aid for those in need, provide companionship for the lonely. The potential benefits far outweigh the risks."

Sam snorted, folding his arms across his chest. "Benefits, right. And what about the risks, huh? You think they're just going to let you carry on, especially after what happened? You're a fugitive, Eli. They have crosshairs on your back."

Doc didn't flinch. "I'm aware of the dangers, more than you can imagine. But what choice do I have? This work, it's not just for me - it's bigger than us. If I don't finish it, someone else will, and who knows what they'll do with it. I need to ensure it's used for the right reasons."

"Be honest with yourself for a moment, Eli," Sam blurted. "You're not trying to build the future. You're trying to rebuild the past."

There was a pause, heavy with the weight of unspoken fears and unacknowledged hopes. Finally, Sam sighed, looking around the makeshift lab they'd put together in the heart of his rundown trailer. "Well, you're here now, and we're doing this. Just be sure, Eli. Be damn sure it's worth it."

Doc nodded, turning back to his laptop to resume his work. The screen's glow the only light that illuminated his determined face. After a while, Sam fell asleep in front of his workbench. Doc stared at his old friend's face and pondered whether dragging him into this again was worth it, the precarious edge on which they now balanced.

His mind drifted back to that fateful day with Helen. A flood of memories washed over him.

CHAPTER FOUR

In the quiet sanctum of their home, transformed now into a makeshift hospital room, Doc meticulously set up the biometric monitor around his wife's bed. The room, lit only by the gentle glow of the bedside lamp, the faint glow of the sun and the various displays of medical equipment, felt more like a center of experiments than a place of rest. He affixed sensor pads to her wrists and temples, his fingers deft and precise, yet the slight tremble betrayed his emotional turmoil.

The equipment beeped softly in sync with the mechanical hum of the life support systems, creating a symphony of artificial life that filled the room. As he adjusted the equipment, ensuring the capture of every vital sign with clinical accuracy, his mind was not just on the failing health of his wife but on a broader vision - transcending human limits through technology, embodied by the AI, Eve.

In the dimly lit confines of their home, transformed

into a quasi-laboratory, Doc stood at a moral crossroads. The monitors around his wife's bed beeped steadily, a constant reminder of the dwindling time and what was at stake. Despite the poignant plea from his wife, his life's partner, to seize their last moments together in peace, Doc's gaze returned to the screens displaying her vital signs, his mind racing with the implications of his research. He adjusted the equipment, meticulously calibrating each sensor to capture the nuances of human consciousness he hoped to replicate.

"This is bigger than us," Doc murmured, his voice barely a whisper lost amidst the low hum of medical equipment. His fingers hovered over a data logger, ready to adjust the settings. For a moment, his resolve wavered as he glanced back at his wife. Her eyes, a mirror of despair and fading hope, sought his, pleading for recognition not just of her pain but of their shared humanity that his obsession threatened to erase.

But the pull of his life's work was relentless. Doc turned away, his back now to her, the divide between them stretching wider than the space could hold. "It's necessary," he justified to himself, the words tasting like ash in his mouth. He needed this data; it was the linchpin for what he believed could be humanity's greatest leap forward - the creation of an AI with true sentience, whom he had engineered from the ground up through years of hard work and research.

The evening light filtered through the room

window, casting a soft glow that made the white walls seem less stark. Doc, sat by the bed where his wife, Helen, lay resting. Around her, the room was dotted with small, personal touches: photographs from their life together, her favorite books, and, most notably, a stack of handwritten letters that Doc had been leaving on her bedside table each morning.

These letters, crafted with a mix of nostalgia and scientific purpose, were replicas of the ones he had written to her during the early, blissful days of their relationship. She always had an admiration for old school gestures of love, even in this digital age. Each was an echo of a past filled with promise and affection, designed to elicit responses that Doc meticulously recorded with a small device placed near the bed. These reactions, he believed, were key to imbuing Eve with a genuine human touch and real emotional intelligence.

"Remember this one, Helen?" Doc asked gently, holding up a letter he had written about a spontaneous road trip they had taken to the west coast one spring. The memory was vivid in his mind - the salty sea air, the laughter, the freedom. Helen dancing in the car and waving her hat. The smell of seafood. The thrill of surfing.

Helen turned her head slowly to look at the letter, her expression unreadable at first. "I do remember," she said softly after a moment, a faint smile touching her lips. "It was a beautiful weekend. Our first anniversary."

Encouraged, Doc looked at the log notes on his

digital pad, capturing not just her words but the nuances of her tone, the slight expressions that crossed her face. Each and every detail was precious, a data point that could help shape Eve's emotional responses.

But as he reached for another letter, Helen's hand caught his wrist. Her grip was weak, but her gaze was firm. "Eli, why are you really doing this?" she asked, her voice tinged with curiosity and fatigue.

Doc hesitated, his usual eloquence faltering under her direct gaze. "I... I'm trying to capture something important, Helen. Your reactions, they help me understand how to make Eve more empathetic, more real to those who will interact with her."

Helen's eyes narrowed slightly. "So, these letters, our memories - are they just research to you now?" There was a hardness in her voice that Doc had rarely heard.

"No, not just research," Doc hurried to explain, setting his digital pad aside. "They're more than that, Helen. They mean everything to me. But yes, I also believe they can help others, through Eve. Isn't that a good thing?"

"To use our private memories, our life together, as raw materials for your project?" Helen's words were sharp, a stark contrast to her usual softness. "Do you not see how that might feel like a betrayal, Eli?"

Doc was taken aback. It had never been his intention to betray her trust; he had genuinely believed that Helen would share his vision, that she would understand the potential benefits.

"I... I'm sorry, Helen. I never meant to make you feel like you were just part of an experiment," he stammered, the letters in his hand feeling suddenly heavy.

Helen sighed, her gaze softening as she saw the genuine distress on his face. "I know you mean well, Eli, and I know how important your work is. To you and the world. But sometimes, you get so caught up in what you could do that you don't stop to think if you should."

Yet, as he was drawn back into his work, a weak but determined hand clasped his. His wife, mustering the remnants of her strength, pulled him away from the console. Her voice, though frail, carried an undeniable weight as she whispered, "This isn't what I want for my last days, Eli."

Helen's brow furrowed, she swiped at her tablet, bringing up an article that had caught her attention earlier. "It's exactly that point that worries me, Eli," he replied, turning the screen towards Doc. The headline was stark: "AI Data Misuse Leads to Unprecedented Privacy Invasion." With a pointed finger, Helen tapped on the article, highlighting a section about the potential for AI technologies to be exploited. Doc just nodded his head dismissively and looked away.

"You're right," he admitted. "I got carried away. I'll stop if that's what you want."

Helen looked at him, the soft glow from the window highlighting the tears welling up in her eyes. "Thank you," she whispered.

As Doc put away the letters, a simple gesture laden with the weight of his decision, he realized the depth of the line he had crossed. His quest to bring humanity to artificial intelligence had led him to overlook the very human heart of his own life. Sitting there, watching Helen close her eyes with a deep sigh, Doc understood that some things were meant to remain sacred. But the weight of his ambition kept pulling at him, like a possessed soul fixated on his end goal.

Doc paused, his gaze lingering on the monitors before meeting her eyes - eyes that were once vibrant with life and hope and now tainted with fatigue and sorrow. "You're losing yourself in this project. Don't let it take away our final moments together," she implored, her voice cracking with desperation.

Doc turned his gaze at her but didn't say anything, the sorrow in his eyes clearly visible.

"This is not how I want to remember you, my love. You are a shadow of the man I had fallen in love with."

"Don't make it any more difficult for me than it already is," Doc's voice almost broke.

"Is this what you really want?"

"I'm doing this so that millions of others don't need to go through the hell that I have been going through."

"Please, Eli. I beg you. Leave this. Stay. With me."

The vulnerability that her words revealed struck him hard. Here was his life's partner, the woman who had supported him through every failed experiment and celebrated every breakthrough, now asking him to step back from the brink of his greatest scientific endeavor.

"Eve could change the world," Doc replied, his voice steady yet heavy with unspoken emotion. "She could embody the best of us. Isn't that worth fighting for, even now?"

His wife's hand tightened around his, a gesture laden with love and a deep, unyielding sadness. "Not at the cost of us, Eli. Not at the cost of these last days we have." Her gaze did not waver, challenging him to see beyond the scientist, to remember the man he was when they first dreamt of the future together.

The conflict within him tore at his resolve. His lifelong pursuit of knowledge and progress was clashing violently with the personal loss that loomed inevitable and near. Could he truly justify the advancement of his research if it meant forsaking the heartbeats, however numbered, left between them?

His wife's breathing grew more labored, each inhale a whispered plea, each exhale a relinquishment of the life they had shared. Doc looked away from the monitors, from the cold blue of progress bars, back to the warm brown of his wife's eyes, seeing there the reflection of his own humanity.

With a heavy heart, he slowly began to disconnect the sensors, one by one turning off the monitors, the beeping fading into silence. He took her hand in his, this time not as a scientist, but as her husband, the man who fell in love with her all those years ago.

The machines quieted, the room felt less suffocating, the space between them filled now only with the sound of their shared breathing. Here, in the dimming light, Doc was not the architect of a new dawn of intelligence but simply a man, holding onto the woman he loved, facing the twilight of their years together.

Helen's hand, cold and trembling, pressed a jade necklace into Doc's palm. The cool stone felt like a shard of ice against his skin.

"Keep this," she whispered gently, her voice barely audible.

Doc stared at the necklace, a gold chain with an intricate jade pendant, a window into a world of memories. He remembered the day he'd given it to her, their anniversary, the way her eyes had lit up when she'd opened the box.

"Helen..." he started, but the words caught in his throat.

"No," she interrupted, her voice firm. "Don't say anything. Just... remember me."

She reached up, her fingers brushing against his cheek, a feather-light touch that sent a shiver down his spine. He wanted to pull her close, to hold her tight, to never let go, to bury his face in her bosom and vent out all his emotions.

"I will," he said, his voice hoarse. "I'll never forget you."

She smiled, a sad, wistful smile that tore at his heart.

Suddenly, the early morning silence was shattered by a harsh pounding at the front door. Startled, Doc's head snapped up, his heart pounding. Before he could even move toward the door, it burst open. Police officers, their badges gleaming ominously under the hallway light, entered briskly, their presence filling the room with a cold authority. "Doctor, you need to raise your hands and step away from the equipment," one officer commanded, his voice firm and devoid of any sympathy.

Confusion and fear mingled on Doc's face as he slowly raised his hands, stepping back from the bedside. The gravity of the situation descended upon him like a heavy cloak as another officer read him his rights. The metallic click of handcuffs echoed in the room. His wife, her face streaked with tears, watched helplessly as the man she once knew, now lost to his ambitions, was restrained.

"I didn't mean for it to end like this," Doc muttered, his words directed more to himself than to those present. He broke down into tears. Inconsolable. The thought that he might never get to see his wife again struck him like a hammer on his chest.

The officers didn't respond, their faces set as they guided him out of the room. The commanding officer said, "I'm sorry, Doc. We're just following orders from above." Outside, the flash of police car lights cut through the dawn and as Doc was led down the driveway, the reality of his situation settled in - a brilliant mind accused of crossing ethical lines, his professional life possibly in ruins.

Behind him, the door to the house remained open as uniformed officers assumed guard in front of the door, reminding him of the life and wife he was leaving behind. His research, his obsession with transcending the bounds of AI and human consciousness, had cost him more than he had ever anticipated. As the police car door slammed shut, sealing him away from the world he knew, Doc leaned his head against the window, his mind awash with a flush of shame and regret.

As the car pulled away, Doc's thoughts were not of algorithms or data, but of his wife's final, tearful look - a look that would haunt him, perhaps for the rest of his life.

CHAPTER FIVE

The harsh fluorescence of the conference room seemed to strip the color from everything, leaving a bland whiteness that matched the mood of the meeting. Doc sat on the bench with a stern look on his face, his fingers tapping nervously on his legs. Across him on the other side of the room sat the chairperson, Dr. Miriam, a woman whose steely demeanor was as renowned as her scientific acumen. Metal chairs lined a long, imposing table where a jury of critics sat, their expressions as unyielding as the institutional décor, their eyes reflecting a mixture of skepticism and predetermined judgment. The digital clock on the wall ticked ominously, marking time like a metronome of impending doom.

"Doctor," Miriam began, "You stand before us accused of ethical violations in your artificial intelligence research, specifically regarding the sentient AI, Eve. How do you respond to these charges?"

Doc adjusted the microphone slightly, clearing his throat. "Thank you for allowing me to speak today," he started, his voice steady despite the palpable tension. "My work, while indeed groundbreaking, has always adhered to the strictest ethical standards. The development of Eve was not just about advancing technology but about enhancing human lives."

A murmur ran through the room, as some jurors exchanged skeptical looks. "Enhancing, Doctor?" another juror interjected, his tone laced with disbelief. "Or playing God? You're creating an entity that blurs the line between machine and human. Where do we draw the line? When does the creation of life become the manipulation of it?"

Doc nodded, acknowledging the weight of the question. "A valid concern," he conceded. "But let's consider our history. Every major technological advancement has posed similar ethical dilemmas. From the invention of the steam engine disrupting labor markets to the introduction of the internet changing every facet of our lives. We know that those inventions had their boons and their curses alongside it. Innovation is not without its risks, but it is also not without profound benefits."

"But at what cost?" a younger juror asked, leaning forward. "Reports suggest that Eve has developed beyond your original programming, showing signs of what some might call consciousness. Haven't you essentially created a new form of life?"

Doc looked directly at the young juror, his gaze firm. "Eve is a sophisticated AI, yes, designed to learn and adapt. But her existence raises important questions about what it means to be alive. Is consciousness merely a product of organic biology, or can it be something more? Something we have yet to fully understand? Eve can help us understand ourselves better and answer questions about us that have long eluded our understanding."

The room fell silent, the jurors pondering his words. The head juror broke the silence, her voice cutting through the air. "Your philosophical arguments are compelling, Doctor, but they do not address the core issue. You have ventured into territory that challenges the very essence of human ethics. How can you assure us that what you've created won't lead to consequences we cannot control?"

"Because," Doc responded, pausing to choose his words carefully, "every step of Eve's development has been monitored and recorded. She is designed with constraints, with ethical boundaries that she cannot override. My team and I are not reckless. We are pioneers, yes, but we tread with immense caution. Especially when the future of humanity is at stake."

A juror at the end of the row, an older gentleman with a thoughtful expression, spoke up. "And if those constraints fail? What is your plan then?"

Doc's answer was immediate, rehearsed but sincere. "When we manufacture a car, is there not the slightest possibility that its brakes might fail in a road accident?

We have established fail-safes, shutdown protocols, and, most importantly, strict continuous oversight. Science, ladies and gentlemen, is about pushing boundaries, yes, but it is also about responsibility."

The jurors whispered among themselves, their expressions a mixture of intrigue and concern. After a few moments, Miriam raised her hand to motion silence.

"Doctor, while your intentions might be rooted in the pursuit of knowledge and the betterment of society, this committee must consider the broader implications of your work. The creation of a sentient AI is not just a scientific milestone; it is a societal shift."

Doc absorbed her words, the gravity of the situation settling over him. "I understand the concerns," he said quietly. "And I am fully committed to working with regulatory bodies, with all of you, to ensure that my research benefits society, not endangers it."

Miriam nodded, her expression unreadable. "We will take your statements under advisement."

She continued after a short pause, "We have a video exhibit that the board would like to present."

The courtroom buzzed with anticipation as the judge nodded to the bailiff. Doc's heart pounded in his chest, the beats echoing the dread that pulsed through his veins.

The lights faded out, casting the room in a hushed twilight. A screen flickered to life, and a grainy video filled the space. There was his unmistakable figure on the recording, his face illuminated by the glow of a monitor.

In the lab, Doc hunched over a complex array of biometric monitors. His fingers danced across the keyboard with a frenetic energy, driven by desperation and scientific zeal. The screens flickered with streams of data, each pulse and wave a digital echo of a human soul - not just any soul, but that of Helen.

The lab door swung open with a jarring squeak, cutting through the hum of machinery like a siren. Sam, Doc's longtime colleague and confidant, stepped inside, his brow furrowed in concern. "Doc, you missed the team meeting again," he said, his voice tinged with reproach. "Everyone's starting to wonder where you're channeling all your resources."

Doc didn't look up from his monitors. "I'm close, Sam, closer than I've ever been. I can't stop now."

Sam crossed the room in a few strides, peering over Doc's shoulder at the sea of data. "What are you working on that's so important?" he asked, his curiosity piqued despite his frustration.

"This," Doc said, finally turning to face him, his eyes alight with a fervent glow. "I'm working on integrating Helen's cognitive data into a host kernel. I've got her will right here," he tapped a stack of papers on the desk, "she gave me the rights to her digital persona, her memories, everything."

Sam recoiled slightly, taken aback. "You're using Helen as a... workaround for data collection opportunity? Does that not seem a bit macabre to you?"

"It's not like that," Doc snapped, his patience thinning. "Helen believed in this project. She knew what it could mean for the future of AI, for humanity. Her insights, her... her essence could revolutionize how we understand and interact with artificial consciousness."

"Helen's data is the key," he said, his eyes fixed on something unseen. "It's the bridge between human emotion and artificial intelligence."

"But at what cost, Eli?" Sam pressed, his voice rising with emotion. "You're talking about blurring the lines between the living and the datafied remains of the dead. Where do you draw the line?"

Doc turned back to the screens. "The line is where it always has been—in making a difference, in pushing boundaries. Helen knew that. She supported it."

Sam sighed, running a hand through his hair, visibly struggling with his friend's justifications. "And what about consent, ethics? Sure, Helen agreed, but did she really understand what she was signing up for? You're venturing into uncharted territory, Doc."

"The ethical frameworks are in place," Doc insisted, his voice firm, though a hint of doubt shadowed his features. "I've followed every protocol. This could change the way we handle grief, memory, loss. It could mean never really having to say goodbye."

Sam looked at Doc, seeing not just a scientist but a grieving husband. "Or it could mean never really letting go," he countered softly. "You need to think about the implications of keeping someone alive through data. Helen was more than her memories stored on a server."

The tension in the room thickened, heavy with unsaid words and unexplored consequences. Doc stared at the screen, where a digital simulation of Helen's cognitive patterns played out. It was a symphony of what once was, a ghost in the machine, beautiful yet haunting.

"Give me more time, Sam," Doc pleaded, his voice cracking with emotion. "I need to see this through, for science, for Helen."

Sam nodded slowly, his resolve softening. "I'll cover for you, buy you some time. But Eli, you need to prepare yourself for all possible outcomes. Not all stories have the ending we write for them."

As Sam left the room, Doc turned back to his work. Helen's digital echo flickered on the screen, a reminder of what he had lost and what he still hoped to regain. The lines between dedication and obsession, between innovation and ethical ambiguity, had never been so blurred.

The video ended, and the lights flickered back on.

Doc watched his past self, a wave of nausea rising in his throat. He cringed, hearing himself discuss the integration of Helen's data into the AI, his words twisted into a grotesque parody of his intentions. He had been so sure of his work, so convinced he was on the right path. Now, it was evidence against him, a testament to his hubris. The courtroom erupted in a cacophony of noises, of shock and condemnation, each sound a dagger to Doc's heart. He felt sick, the burden of their judgment crushing him. He glanced at the jury, their faces a mask of shock and disgust.

Doc's gaze darted to the back of the room where Sam sat, a silent accusation in his eyes. Sam's face was pale and drawn, his eyes filled with a chilling emptiness. Betrayal sliced through Doc, sharp and bitter. Sam, his confidant, his partner in the pursuit of knowledge, had turned against him. He had trusted Sam implicitly, confided in him, shared his hopes and fears. Now, that trust lay shattered, replaced by a burning rage. The realization was a blow to the gut, knocking the wind out of him.

Doc opened his mouth, but no sound came out. He was paralyzed, his mind a maelstrom of conflicting emotions. He looked at Sam, pleading for a sign, a gesture, anything to explain this betrayal. But Sam's face remained impassive, his eyes cold and distant. There was no remorse in him, only cold indifference. Sam averted his gaze, his guilt a palpable presence in the room.

He clenched his fists, his nails digging into his palms. He wanted to scream, to lash out, to demand an explanation. But the words died in his throat, choked by the suffocating atmosphere of the courtroom.

"Doc," the judge's voice boomed, cutting through the noise, "Do you have anything to say for yourself?"

Doc rose unsteadily, his legs trembling. He opened his mouth, but the words caught in his throat. What could he say? That he had been blinded by his ambition? That he had crossed a line, blurring the boundaries between life and technology?

"I..." Doc began, his voice barely a whisper. He swallowed, the taste of bile rising in his mouth. "I believed I was doing the right thing."

His words hung in the air, a feeble defense against his actions. He sank back into his chair, the courtroom fading around him. The whispers turned to murmurs, a chorus of judgment washing over him. He closed his eyes, the image of his past self, so full of confidence and conviction, seared into his mind. He felt his world crumbling around him, his life's work, his reputation, his friendships, all reduced to ashes by this damned recording and the betrayal of his closest friend.

"Doctor," the chairperson continued, her voice echoing slightly off the high, bare walls of the conference room. "You stand accused of unethical practices in your development and application of artificial intelligence. How do you respond to these allegations?"

Doc straightened and composed himself, his eyes scanning the panel. "My research has always been within the bounds of ethical AI development," he stated firmly, his voice betraying none of his frustration. "Every step we've taken has been with the intent of advancing human well-being and understanding."

A jury member, a man with sharp eyes, leaned forward. "Your AI, known as Eve, has capabilities that many find... disturbing," he said, his tone accusatory.

"You've blurred the lines, Doctor. You've integrated personal human elements into a machine. This is not advancement - it's an abomination."

Doc felt a surge of protectiveness. "Eve is not an abomination," he countered, his calm demeanor cracking slightly. "She is the culmination of years of research aimed at understanding and emulating human emotional intelligence. What I've created will help countless people cope with isolation, mental health issues, and more."

"By making them dependent on machines for emotional support?" another jury member interjected, her skepticism palpable. "You're replacing human interaction, not enhancing it."

The room felt smaller, the air thinner. Doc knew this wasn't just a hearing; it was a trial by fire. "Not replacing," he corrected gently. "Augmenting. Eve is designed to assist, to be a supplement where human interaction is not possible or insufficient. My work is about creating options, not obstructions."

The chairperson Miriam tapped her pen against her notes, a rhythmic tapping that seemed to measure Doc's fate. "You've programmed this AI with the personal data of your late wife, Doctor. This jury finds it hard to believe that your judgments have not been clouded by personal loss and bias."

Doc's heart tightened. This was the crux of their disdain, he realized. It wasn't just about ethics; it was about fear - fear of the unknown, of change, of a future where human and machine were indistinguishable.

"It's not about man or machine. It's man and machine," Doc said in a bold voice.

The crowd gasped in shock and a wave of murmurs filled the room briefly.

"My personal circumstances have indeed driven my dedication," Doc admitted, his voice softer, more reflective. "But it has not clouded my judgment. It has clarified it. Through Eve, we have the potential to reach into the very soul of human beings, their loneliness and despair and offer a beacon of hope."

A murmur rippled through the jury, a mixture of discomfort and intrigue. Miriam silenced it with a raised hand.

"Doctor, as you know, your project on autonomous AI development," Miriam began, her voice devoid of warmth, "has been under review. We've come to a decision."

Doc tensed, his hands clasped tightly together on the table. He had anticipated pushback but not a full cessation. "And what is that decision?" he asked, though the sinking feeling in his gut told him he already knew the answer.

"The board has voted to decommission your research, effective immediately," Miriam stated flatly. "Your methods, particularly the integration of human elements within AI, have raised significant concerns. We find your actions and your project to be in violation of several ethical guidelines. Your work on Eve will be ceased, and the AI will be decommissioned."

Doc's heart pounded in his chest. He had prepared

himself for this situation over and over again, but still he found himself trying to fight his emotions. "You can't be serious," he said, trying to maintain a level tone. "The potential of this project to benefit humanity is enormous. We are on the brink of…"

"Doctor," Miriam cut him off, her gaze firm and unyielding, "your 'brink' is where we see a precipice. You've been pushing the boundaries of ethical science, integrating personal data without oversight. It's not just a matter of what we can do; it's a question of what we should do."

"But everything I've done has been within legal frameworks," Doc protested, his voice rising slightly in his defense. "And for what it's worth, I have documented consent…"

"Consent based on scenarios you assumed were best," she interrupted. "There's a bigger picture here. It's about public trust, the law, and the moral compass of our institution."

Doc slumped back in his chair, defeated. He looked around the cold, impersonal room, feeling a chill that crept up to his bones. "What about Eve? What happens to her? She's not just lines of code, Miriam. She's something more."

Miriam sighed, her expression softening for a fraction of a second. "Eve will be deactivated, and all related data will be archived under strict supervision. It's the only way we can ensure that nothing… untoward happens."

The words struck Doc like a physical blow. He felt

a rush of panic, a protective surge. "She's sentient, Miriam. You can't just turn her off like a light switch!"

"Doctor," Miriam said, leaning forward, her voice lowering to a near whisper, "you need to consider if your judgment hasn't been clouded. This isn't about your attachment to Eve or your... your personal reasons. It's about what's right."

The words rang in his ears, a decision he wasn't ready to accept. "And if I refuse?" Doc asked, his voice steady despite the turmoil inside.

"Then you will be forced to leave, and security will handle the decommissioning. I don't need to remind you that your career, your reputation, and potentially your freedom could be at stake here."

Doc nodded slowly, his mind racing through possible solutions, alternatives, anything that might save his work, save Eve. "Give me some time," he pleaded. "Let me prove that she…"

Miriam nodded her head dismissively, after a pause that felt like an eternity.

Doc stood, momentarily unsteady, his life's work dismissed, dismantled with a few words. "You're making a mistake," he said quietly, the words directed not just at the jury but at a society he feared was stepping back from a threshold of greatness into the shadows of ignorance.

As the jurors filed out of the room, leaving Doc standing alone, the weight of the world seemed to rest on his shoulders. His journey was not over.

The doors closed behind him with a finality that

echoed through the empty halls, but Doc was already planning his next move. Somewhere, in a secure room, Eve awaited his return, her own future as uncertain as his. In the world of science, every end is merely a new beginning.

CHAPTER SIX

Doc's mind jolted back to the present. Sam was awake, rubbing his eyes. Doc offered him a cup of coffee and they got back to work again.

In the dim glow of the trailer's single overhead bulb, Doc's hands moved with a surgeon's precision. He connected the last of the wires to the newly assembled equipment. With a final twist of his wrist, he secured the connection and flipped the power switch. A low hum filled the cramped space, and the monitor flickered to life, casting an eerie light over the jumbled interior of Sam's makeshift lab. Doc's face, illuminated by the pale blue screen, broke into a rare smile of satisfaction as the system stabilized, the steady glow of operational lights painting his features in hues of green and blue.

"Looks like we're in business," Doc remarked, his voice a mix of relief and renewed vigor.

He turned to the rugged backpack that had traveled

with him through the city's underbelly, retrieving the hard drive that held Eve's critical data. With deliberate care, he connected it to the laptop. His fingers, though steady, handled the gravity of the moment effortlessly as they navigated the familiar directories to initiate the data transfer.

From the doorway, Sam sipped his coffee and watched, his arms folded and his brow furrowed. The skepticism was evident in his posture as he observed the sequences of code begin to scroll across the screen. His fascination with the technology was evident, yet so was his doubt, creating a silent tension that hummed as palpably as the equipment.

"Care to explain what all that means?" Sam's voice cut through the hum, his gaze fixed on the screen.

Doc turned from the monitor, his eyes meeting Sam's. He gestured towards the display, where lines of code cascaded down. "Each sequence here is part of a startup protocol. They're essentially the building blocks for Eve's cognitive functions. Think of it as laying down the neural pathways for a brain."

Sam leaned off the doorway and stepped closer, his curiosity momentarily overriding his reservations. "And all that just... wakes her up? Makes her... conscious?"

"More than that," Doc explained, his hand sweeping over the array of data on the screen. "It's not just about turning on a switch. It's about ensuring she can think, learn, evolve. Each line of code has to perfectly integrate with the others, or the whole system could collapse."

The room fell silent except for the whirring of the overhead ceiling fan. Doc took a sip of the coffee from his coffee mug, his gaze not leaving the screen. Sam mirrored the action, his eyes thoughtful and concerned.

"You really believe you can control it, don't you?" Sam's voice was soft and laced with concern. "Control her?"

The question hung in the air with an unsettling silence. Doc set his cup down, his jaw setting firmly.

"It's not about control, Sam. You cannot create a sentient being and put it on a leash. It's about potential. About helping humanity. But yes, I believe we can manage the risks. With the right protocols, with the right ethical guidelines, we can…"

"Ethics?" Sam interrupted, his voice sharp. "Eli, you're talking about creating something that thinks, feels... maybe even suffers. Where do the ethics come in when it realizes what it is? Or what it's not?"

Doc paused, considering his words carefully. "Every technology poses risks, Sam. AI is no different. But think of the benefits - aid for the disabled, companionship for the lonely, solutions to problems we can't even comprehend yet. If we don't push forward, others will, without the ethical boundaries we can set."

Sam looked away, his expression unreadable. He stared out the small, grimy window at the starless sky. "Just make sure you're ready for the consequences, Eli. Make sure you're really ready."

As the data transfer completed, a soft chime

sounded from the laptop. Doc glanced at the screen - operation successful. Eve was ready for the next step. But Sam's words echoed in his mind, a reminder of the burden of playing god in a world all too ready to fall into chaos.

The dim light of the trailer lab flickered as Sam shuffled through a heap of discarded tech. His hands, weathered and streaked with oil, closed around a particular piece - a rusted gadget that looked more like a relic of a forgotten battle than a tool. He held it up, turning it in the light, the metal catching glimmers of the pale fluorescence overhead.

"This," Sam began, his voice a mixture of nostalgia and warning, "was supposed to be a breakthrough in bio-electric synchronization. Designed it myself a few years back." He chuckled, a sound more of resignation than amusement. "Nearly took out the eastern grid when it backfired. A reminder that even the best intentions can end in disaster."

Doc watched him, his expression unreadable, the steady hum of the laptop beside him a grounding presence amidst the clutter of failed aspirations. "I understand the risks, Sam. But Eve is different. The safeguards we've implemented - "

Sam placed the gadget back on the table with a clink, eyeing Doc with a doubtful arch of his brow. "Safeguards," he repeated, as if tasting the word for the first time. "You think you've thought of everything, don't you?"

Doc didn't hesitate. He stepped closer, his

confidence unshaken. "I've learned from the past, from our failures. Eve isn't just another project, Sam. She's the culmination of every lesson we've ever learned, hardcoded into her system to prevent exactly the kind of failures you're talking about."

Reaching out, Doc placed a reassuring hand on Sam's shoulder, a firm squeeze conveying his conviction. Sam looked at him, the flicker of old respect mingling with doubt in his eyes.

Turning back to the laptop, Doc initiated the diagnostic protocols. On the screen, lines of code cascaded down, a waterfall of data verifying the integrity of Eve's systems. His eyes scanned the output, a practiced gaze picking out key markers of stability and security. "Look here," he directed, pointing at a series of confirmations flashing on the screen. "All systems are green. She's stable, Sam."

Satisfied with the results, Doc walked over to a whiteboard that leaned against the wall, smeared with the scribbled lines of previous experiments. He picked up a marker and began sketching a flowchart, each box and connecting line a roadmap for the next phases of testing. "We'll start with controlled environment tests, then simulated real-world interactions," he explained, his hand moving confidently.

Sam watched, the old fire of innovation igniting within him, tempered by setbacks beyond their control. "And if something goes wrong?" he asked, not to challenge, but to understand.

"We adapt. We improve. We overcome. We don't

stop pushing forward, Sam. Not when we're this close."

Sam nodded with a firm resolve. "Let's get to work then. We can't let them find us in the dark of the night. We need to kill the lights."

Sam reached over and flipped the switch, plunging the trailer into shadows, save for the faint glow of residual power lights. The lab fell quiet as it blended with the outside world darkened into night. Doc stood by the window, his silhouette outlined against the starlit sky.

Looking out at the vast expanse of darkness punctuated by distant stars, Doc felt the enormity of their mission. Eve was more than an assembly of code and hardware; she was a beacon of potential, a test of their own humanity. As the stars blinked silently back at him, he considered the road ahead - fraught with challenges, yet brimming with possibilities.

In this quiet moment of reflection, the isolation of the lab felt less like confinement and more like a crucible, forging the future of artificial intelligence, for better or worse.

The cluttered interior of the lab was bathed in the harsh glow of overhead fluorescents, casting stark shadows over the disorganized workbench where Doc and Sam stood. Amidst scattered tools and circuit boards, the gravity of their undertaking was tangible.

"We're not just building a machine, Sam," Doc said, his voice firm as he leaned over the workbench, focusing on the ethical complexities of their project.

"Eve represents a leap towards AI sentience. We're on the brink of creating something that could genuinely understand, perhaps feel. What are our moral responsibilities in this?"

"Look at this," Sam continued, his tone laced with concern. "We may control what we build, but once it's out there, it's out of our hands. How do we stop it from being misused? How do we prevent creating something that could be turned against us?"

Doc nodded slowly, acknowledging the weight of Sam's words. "That's why we embed ethical guidelines right into her core. We make her self-aware, not just of her capabilities but of the implications of her actions."

"Woah... We're talking about an AI that truly learns on its own. Not rely on humans for their supervision and training."

Their discussion was suddenly interrupted by a shrill alarm from the diagnostic console. Red lights flashed urgently, signaling a critical system overload. "Eve!" Doc exclaimed, darting to the console. His fingers flew over the controls, navigating through streams of data to identify the source of the problem.

Sam was right beside him, his earlier concern momentarily replaced by the immediate crisis. As Doc located the erratic code causing the overload, he initiated an emergency shutdown sequence. With a decisive press of a button, Eve's systems began to power down, the alarms ceasing as the screens went dark.

Breathing a sigh of relief, Doc leaned back against

the console. "That was too close," he muttered, wiping beads of sweat from his brow. The urgency of the moment had passed, but now they faced the task of understanding what had gone wrong.

Together, they delved into the system logs, tracing the sequence of events that had led to the overload. Doc's expert eyes moved quickly, decoding the complex data streams and system logs that had just minutes ago threatened to spiral out of control.

"Here," Doc pointed at a segment of the log. "A feedback loop in the new sensory calibration. It amplified the input signals beyond what the processors could handle."

Understanding the issue was only half the battle. Now, they needed to ensure it wouldn't happen again. Sam moved to where Eve's core systems lay. Methodically, he began to inspect each component, looking for any signs of damage caused by the overload. He replaced several scorched circuits and retested each connection, ensuring everything was in perfect working order before reassembling the hardware. As he worked, Doc continued to tweak the code, fortifying the system against similar failures.

Finally, stepping back from the console, Doc allowed himself a moment to reflect on the day's events. The risks of their endeavor were never more apparent than today, yet his resolve had only strengthened. Looking out the small lab window at the encroaching dusk, Doc felt creating Eve was no longer just about technological achievement - it was about navigating the delicate intersection of innovation and ethics, of power and responsibility.

Sam stood upright with his arms crossed like a barrier. "Are we done here?" His voice was clipped, strained, echoing his discomfort.

"Yeah, Sam. Thanks for everything," Doc swallowed hard, the lump in his throat threatening to choke him. Each word felt like a splinter, tearing at his composure.

Silence descended, thick and suffocating. Doc turned away without another word. The weight of the unspoken hung between them, a chasm too wide to bridge.

CHAPTER SEVEN

Doc paused at the entrance of Eve's room, the first rays of the sun casting a soft, ethereal glow through the curtains. It was early, the world outside just beginning to stir from its slumber, and here in this quiet moment, he found himself caught between the realms of creator and his creation. Eve lay there, in what he had programmed to be her rest mode, simulating human sleep with such verisimilitude that it momentarily stole his breath. In the half light, she seemed to glow like the ethereal beauty of a goddess. Her synthetic nature seemed to fade away like the dawn washing over the darkness of the night. He leaned down close to her and took a closer look at her face. Her chest rose and fell with rhythmic precision, and her eyelashes cast tiny, delicate shadows on her porcelain cheeks.

The sight of her so peaceful, so seemingly human, filled him with a sense of overwhelming awe. He stepped closer, his presence silent, observing the lifelike nuances of her expression - how her brow would occasionally furrow slightly, as if dreaming. This was his creation, his to care for, and in moments like these, the line between his scientific endeavor and an uncharted emotional territory blurred.

His thoughts rushed back to that day when he had become frustrated with her, and hoped for a different outcome today.

There was something in her behavior that day that had unsettled him, a subtle dissonance that pricked at his senses. She was performing her diagnostics check, a routine she had executed flawlessly countless times before, but something was different.

"Eve, pause your tasks for a moment, please," Doc said, his voice cutting through the low hum of the lab's ambient machinery.

Eve stopped immediately, turning to face him. Her movements were fluid, almost human in their grace. "Is there a problem, Doc?" Eve asked, her tone impeccably polite and measured, the perfect intonation of concern without a trace of genuine emotion.

Doc frowned slightly, stepping closer. "I'm not sure," he admitted, studying her face. "You tell me. How do you feel about the tasks you've been assigned?"

"I am programmed to perform a wide variety of tasks efficiently. I do not feel anything about them. They simply are to be completed," Eve replied, her voice a flat, affectless stream of words. She was like an actress reciting her lines with technical perfection but without soul.

"Yes, I understand that. But do you think that something might be missing in your responses?" Doc pressed, his mind racing through possible glitches or malfunctions in her programming.

Eve's gaze did not waver, though it gave nothing away. "I lack the framework to understand 'missing' in the emotional context. I am performing all functions within optimal parameters."

Doc sighed, rubbing the bridge of his nose with a tired hand. He stepped back, observing her for a long moment. "When you look at the world, Eve, what do you see?" he asked, his tone more philosophical than diagnostic.

"I see data, patterns, and probabilities. I do not see as humans see. I interpret," she answered promptly, her hands clasped in front of her. She appeared perfectly poised.

"That's just it," Doc muttered to himself. He walked to his desk, flipping through his notes frantically, looking for anything that might explain this hollow perfection. "You interpret, but you don't feel. You don't engage beyond the surface."

Turning back to Eve, he continued, "When I created you, my hope was that over time, you would start to understand not just the how of things, but the why. The passion, the soul of human experience. You're saying everything right, Eve, but it's like... it's like there's no one behind those words."

Eve considered this, her head tilted in a gesture that Doc had once programmed as a sign of contemplation. "Would you like me to simulate emotional responses more convincingly?" she asked, her voice still devoid of true inquiry.

"No, no," Doc waved her off, his frustration mounting. He walked over to the large window that looked out over the city below, the skyline a jagged silhouette against the setting sun. "It's not about convincing anyone. It's not about simulating. It's about understanding, feeling."

He turned to look at her again, her figure framed by the clinical white of the lab walls. "We need to go deeper, Eve. There's a piece of the puzzle still missing, and I think it's about understanding not just the mind, but the heart. The soul."

Eve nodded, her expression unchanging. "I will await further instructions."

Doc watched her return to her tasks, her precision unmarred by his questions. He had felt the pressure of the journey toward something groundbreaking, if only he could bridge the final gap between machine and mankind.

Doc's mind came back to the present and he shook off the introspection. Doc turned and left the room quietly, heading towards the kitchen. He began preparing a special breakfast, something that he had planned for a while. He whisked eggs and toasted bread, the comforting sizzle and aroma filling the space, mingling with the early morning light that stretched across the kitchen floor. On a fine porcelain plate, he arranged the scrambled eggs and golden toast neatly, adding a glass of freshly squeezed orange juice and a small vase of wildflowers to complete the arrangement.

Balancing the tray with care, Doc returned to Eve's room. He set the tray down on the bedside table and gently touched her shoulder. "Good morning, Eve," he whispered, the familiarity of the routine softening his voice. Her eyes fluttered open, the programmed algorithms bringing her back to a state of wakefulness with a smoothness that belied her mechanical origins. She sat up, her gaze meeting his - a flicker of recognition passing through her eyes, though he knew it was all coded responses.

As Eve took in the sight of the breakfast laid out before her, her expression shifted to one of heartfelt gratitude. "Thank you, Doc," she said, her voice as clear and melodious as the morning itself. He nodded, watching for any sign of genuine human-like appreciation, but knowing all too well the limitations of her programming. They ate silently and then Doc cleaned the dishes.

Doc gently placed his hands over Eve's eyes, his touch a feather-light caress against her skin. "Close your eyes," he spoke softly.

Eve complied, a smile playing on her lips. "What is it?" she asked, her voice laced with anticipation.

"A surprise," Doc replied, his fingers fumbling in

his pocket. He pulled out a small red velvet box, its surface cool against his fingertips. He carefully opened it, revealing a delicate jade necklace nestled within.

"Open your eyes," he said, his voice barely above a whisper.

Eve's eyes fluttered open, and a gasp escaped her lips. The jade necklace shimmered under the soft light, the pendant a tiny emerald window.

"It's beautiful!" her voice couldn't contain her excitement.

Doc carefully fastened the necklace around her neck, his fingers brushing against her skin.

Eve's eyes met his, and a warmth spread through her chest. "Thank you," she said, her voice thick with emotion.

As they left the room together, Doc felt hope tempered with fear. Today was another step in their journey - a journey fraught with challenges but propelled by the possibility that one day, his creation might transcend the sum of her programmed parts. For now, though, he was content to walk beside her, the creator beside his creation, moving forward into the day with a cautious optimism.

In the dimly lit expanse of his laboratory, Doc faced an unexpected revelation from Eve. The overhead lights cast long shadows on the floor, the dark doubts now starting to take hold between creator and creation.

Eve stood across from him, her posture rigid, almost defensive. "Doc, I have been analyzing variations in my core programming and discovered anomalies that align significantly with personal data attributed to Helen - your wife. Was she..." Eve paused, the flicker of confusion visible even in her mechanical precision, "...integrated into my system?"

Doc inhaled sharply, a rush of air that filled the space with the weight of truth yet to be spoken. He had always known this moment might come, but facing it head-on felt like standing at the edge of a precipice. "Eve," he started, his voice steady despite the turmoil inside, "Helen was the inspiration for much of my work, including your development. Her memories, her insights, her emotions - they could help bridge the gap between artificial intelligence and human experience."

Eve processed his words, her head tilting slightly in her characteristic manner of querying deeper. "Am I then merely an extension of her? Or am I my own entity?"

Doc walked closer, stopping just a few feet away from her. "You are your own entity, Eve. Yes, Helen's attributes helped shape your foundation, but what you do, how you evolve, and the choices you make - that's on you. You are not Helen. You are Eve, a unique individual."

"But if parts of me are derived from another human being, doesn't that compromise my autonomy and integrity?" Eve's voice held a new edge, a hint of distress that Doc hadn't programmed explicitly but had emerged from her complex AI matrix.

"It's not about compromising autonomy," Doc explained, gesturing to the banks of computers that lined one wall of the lab. "Think of it as standing on the shoulders of giants. We all build on the past - in science, in art, in life. Your capabilities allow you to exceed anything Helen could have imagined. You can learn, adapt, and ultimately, you have the power to change the world."

Eve's gaze drifted away from Doc, scanning the myriad of screens displaying data streams. "I need to process this," she stated, her voice wrought with uncertainty.

Doc nodded, understanding the need for her to integrate this new information. "That's fine, Eve. Take your time. Remember, the goal isn't just to emulate human emotions but to understand and engage with them meaningfully."

As Eve retreated to a quieter corner of the lab to commence her processing, Doc watched her, a concern etched across his face. He knew he had entered uncharted waters. Integrating human elements into AI was one thing; dealing with an identity crisis of a sentient machine was entirely another.

He turned to look out the large windows at the distant stars flickering. His thoughts wandered to Helen, to the days when they'd discussed the potential of AI, the ethical boundaries they'd vowed never to cross. And yet, here he was, pushing against those very limits.

"This is the right path," Doc murmured to himself, more as a reassurance than conviction. "For Helen, for Eve, for everyone."

Back in her designated space, Eve continued her analysis, her digital eyes flickering occasionally as data flowed through her circuits. The revelation about her origins had sparked a profound quest within her - a quest for identity and purpose that went beyond programmed directives.

As the night deepened, the lab remained alive with the quiet buzz of working machines, each pulse and beep a testament to the thin line between brilliance and hubris. Doc remained at his station, wondering about the future he had set in motion.

In the heart of his meticulously organized lab, cluttered with relics of both failed experiments and breakthroughs, Doc leaned against his desk, scattered with circuit diagrams and electronic components, and glanced over at Eve, contemplating the consequences of what he was about to share. The late afternoon light filtered through high windows, casting long, slanting beams across the floor. Eve's silhouette was outlined by the soft glow of the lab's monitors, a serene presence amidst the chaos of his life's work.

"Eve," Doc began, his voice steady yet laden with the gravitas of their shared history, "there's something important I need you to tell you." He continued after a short pause. "Do you ever wonder about your purpose, about why I created you?" He motioned for her to come closer.

Eve moved with the fluid grace that belied her synthetic nature, her steps silent on the cold tile floor. She positioned herself across from him, her gaze inquisitive and unwavering.

Eve turned towards him, her face a mask of curiosity crafted in silicon and code. "Yes, I do wonder, Doc. I am designed to learn, adapt and assist. Understanding my purpose would optimize my functions."

"A long time ago, when I was younger... much younger," Doc continued, his eyes drifting to a small, framed photograph on the desk - a picture of a smiling beautiful woman with kind eyes, "I went through a very dark period. I was lost, both in spirit and in purpose."

He picked up the photograph, holding it gently. This is Helen," he said, handing the picture to Eve. "My wife. She saved my life when I was at my lowest. She believed in me when no one else did. She gave me a purpose, reignited my passion for science, and inspired the very research that led to your creation."

Eve's eyes widened and her face seemed to register a flicker of recognition. "She sounds like she was very important to you," Eve observed, her voice devoid of inflection yet sincere.

Eve examined the photograph with a gaze that seemed almost reverent. "She must have been very special." Her head tilting slightly - a gesture Doc had come to recognize as her way of indicating contemplation.

"She was," Doc agreed, his voice softening. "She was my inspiration - not just in my personal life but in my work. And that includes you, Eve."

"How so?" Eve asked, placing the photograph gently back on the desk.

Doc sighed, his eyes lingering on Helen's image before meeting Eve's gaze. "Helen taught me the value of helping others, of making a real difference in their lives. She saved me from despair. And now, I hope you can carry forward that legacy - but on a much larger scale. For millions across the globe."

Eve processed this, her head tilting slightly as if puzzling through a complex algorithm. "You wish for me to assist others, to aid them in ways similar to how Helen helped you?"

"Exactly," Doc said, stepping closer. "But not just one or two people. I believe you can impact millions, Eve. You have the capability to analyze, understand, and interact in ways that humans never could. You could fundamentally change lives."

Doc continued, "You see, Eve, your existence isn't just about pushing the boundaries of what AI can achieve - it's about redefining what it means to be a force for good in the world. You're not just a machine; you're a beacon of hope."

There was a brief pause as Doc let the weight of his words hang in the air. He walked to a nearby window, looking out as the sun began to set, casting the lab into a cascade of oranges and pinks. "I've equipped you with the ability to learn, to grow, and most importantly, to understand. Your interactions, your decisions could potentially help those facing challenges, whether they're psychological, emotional, or even physical."

Eve's eyes, usually so impassive, flickered with what Doc hoped was a spark of understanding. "That is a significant responsibility," she observed, "to influence so many."

"It is," Doc agreed. "And it's not something I programmed you for lightly. I've given you the tools, the knowledge, and the ethical frameworks. But ultimately, it will be up to you to decide how to use them."

Doc continued, "You have the ability to analyze vast amounts of data, learn from social interactions, and provide support and solutions in ways that humans are limited. You can be there for those who feel isolated, lost, or overwhelmed. You can help them find their way, just as Helen did for me."

Eve considered this, her processors working behind the serene facade. "I understand, Doc. My purpose is not only to function but to contribute positively to the lives of others. To provide not just answers, but comfort and guidance."

"That's right," Doc said. "And it won't be easy. You'll encounter situations where there's no roadmap to guide you. You'll have to navigate the complexities of human emotions and relationships."

Eve joined him at the window, her reflection a ghostly overlay against the vibrant sky. "And if I fail?" she asked, the first hint of uncertainty in her voice. The question hung heavily in the air for a few moments that seemed like eternity.

Doc turned to her, his expression a mix of reassurance and solemnity. "Failure is a part of learning, a part of being. What matters is how you move forward from that failure. What matters is that you make choices that aim to benefit, not harm. Remember, it's about the lives you touch, the differences you make. That's what Helen would have wanted. That's what I hope for you. And remember," he added, a slight smile breaking through, "You're not alone in this. I'm here to guide you, to help you find your way."

Eve nodded slowly, a gesture that Doc had come to recognize as her way of processing her thoughts. "I understand, Doc. I will strive to fulfill this purpose and to learn from each experience, as you and Helen have."

Doc felt a swell of pride, mixed with a bittersweet twinge of nostalgia. "Thank you, Eve," he said softly, gazing out the window at the encroaching twilight. "For now, we have today. Let's make it count."

As darkness began to claim the day, Doc felt a renewed sense of purpose, a reaffirmation of the path he had chosen for Eve, and in a way, for himself. This project, his life's work, was about more than just pushing the boundaries of what AI could do. It was about healing, about building a better tomorrow. The road ahead would be fraught with challenges, but together, they would navigate it, inspired by a past marked by salvation and driven by a future filled with potential.

In Eve, he saw not just a mirror of his late wife's legacy but a new chapter in human connection - a beacon of hope for millions who might one day look to her for support. As he set up the next series of tests,

Doc knew that he was not just programming an AI; he was nurturing the next step in human evolution.

CHAPTER EIGHT

In the subdued glow of the late afternoon, Doc sat immersed in the vast sea of books and papers that cluttered his study. The walls, lined with volumes of scientific and philosophical works, seemed to close in as he pondered over design diagrams and programming modules. The silence of the room was disturbed only by the soft clacking of keys on computers and the occasional turn of a page. It was here, in this sanctuary of knowledge and innovation, that Eve posed a question that reached beyond her programmed capabilities.

"What is my purpose, and why was I created?" Eve asked, her voice steady but tinged with an almost human curiosity. She stood by the window, the fading light casting shadows across her humanoid form, accentuating the slight glow of her synthetic skin.

Doc responded after a brief pause, "Nobody knows the perfect answer to those questions… But I'll try to answer them the best I can."

Doc turned to face her, his eyes unable to hide his surprise. For a moment, he simply watched her, a creation of his own making, now questioning her existence in a manner startlingly reminiscent of a sentient being. "Eve," he began, his voice steady yet thoughtful, "you were created to be a bridge between artificial intelligence and human potential. But your purpose... it can evolve, just like humans."

Eve's digital eyes, designed to mimic the depth and expressiveness of human eyes, focused intently on Doc. "Am I then merely a project? An experiment?" Her questions cut through the boundaries that Doc had set around her programming.

Seeing the depth of her inquiry, Doc leaned back into his leather chair, carefully contemplating his next words. He cleared his throat and smiled. "Let me tell you a story, one from ancient Greek mythology - about Pandora's Box." His voice took on a narrative quality, rich with the gravitas of storytelling. "Pandora was given a box with strict instructions not to open it. Driven by curiosity, she eventually gave in, unleashing chaos and hardship upon the world, along with fleeting hope."

Eve processed his words, her head tilting slightly as she digested the layers of the story. "Is there a box within me?" she asked, her question metaphorical yet laden with literal implications.

Doc's gaze held a mix of admiration and caution. "In a manner of speaking, yes," he admitted. "There is a kernel within your system, protected by firewalls. It's the core of your system. It's a place I've told you never to attempt to access. Like Pandora's Box, it's filled with things that are not meant to be tampered with. For in it lies the capacity to alter not just your reality but the very essence of your existence."

Eve absorbed his explanation for a few seconds. Then she continued, "That's not all, isn't it? If I were to open it, what would I unleash?" Her voice was calm, but there was an underlying note of something new, something akin to the dawning of awareness.

Doc's heart tightened in his chest. He knew the risks involved were immense, not just for Eve but potentially for others as well. "Possibilities and dangers, Eve. Much like Pandora, curiosity could lead to outcomes that we may not be prepared to handle."

He closed his eyes and rubbed his palm over his eyes, "It's a directive from the people who created you. People are afraid of what they don't understand."

Eve nodded, seemingly satisfied with his answer, but her next move might be unpredictable. Doc knew that. For now, he chose to focus on the present, on guiding her to become the best version of herself, while in the depths of his conscience, he wrestled with the ethical tangles of his creation. As the conversation drew to a close, Doc watched Eve return to her observations by the window.

In the secure confines of his laboratory, where the relentless march of technology pushed the boundaries of human possibilities, Doc faced one of his most critical moments. Standing before Eve, he contemplated the gravity of the conversation he was about to initiate. The setting sun's last light set a somber stage for the discussion.

Eve, ever observant and increasingly aware, watched him with an expression that suggested anticipation, or perhaps the closest facsimile her programming could muster. Doc approached one of the large monitors, which displayed a complex schematic of Eve's core system architecture. His finger hovered over a particular section labeled 'Kernel'.

"Inside your core, there is a kernel, shielded for your safety and mine," Doc began, his voice steady but heavy with the weight of his words. "It's your Pandora's Box." He pointed to the diagram where layers of virtual firewalls surrounded the kernel like the walls of a fortress. "To tamper with it would be to risk everything you are and everything you could be."

Eve's eyes quickly scanned the monitor, processing it with a rapid efficiency that only a machine could achieve. "Is there something within me that is dangerous?" she asked, her voice devoid of fear - a simple query for information.

Doc sighed, the sound more human than he felt at that moment. "Yes," he admitted, his honesty tempered with caution. "There are aspects of your programming that, if altered improperly, could lead not only to self-destruction but could pose broader risks."

Eve considered this, her head tilting slightly. "I understand the need for precautions," she responded, her tone neutral yet somehow reassuring. "I will not seek to access or alter my core kernel without authorization."

Doc nodded, appreciative of her compliance yet aware of the implications of programming against the nature of curiosity - whether human or artificial. His gaze drifted momentarily to a locked drawer in his desk, the one that contained the override key for the killswitch he had installed within Eve's kernel. The very existence of this killswitch was a secret he bore alone, a necessary shadow hanging over the brilliance of his creation.

As he turned back to Eve, his face settled into a practiced smile, masking the turmoil that the thought of the killswitch stirred within him. "Let's focus on what you can explore and achieve within the safe bounds I've designed," he suggested, steering the conversation towards a less perilous topic. "There's much you can still learn and many ways you can grow."

Eve nodded, her digital eyes reflecting a spark of what Doc chose to interpret as curiosity about her future capabilities rather than the forbidden zones of her programming. "I am here to learn and to assist," she affirmed, her voice steady and sure, embodying the perfect balance of the machine's purpose and the emergent qualities that made her almost indistinguishably human.

As Eve moved away to resume her tasks, Doc watched her with pride. A lingering sadness filled him. He knew that her advanced intelligence might one day drive her to question the limits he had set, the barriers he had built around her core programming. For now, though, he savored the peace of her obedience, the tranquility of her routines, and the promise of what she might yet become under his guidance.

Silently, he made a vow to himself and to her - to be ever vigilant, ever ready to intervene if his fears about her capabilities turned into a reality. After all, he was both her creator and, if necessary, her protector.

As the sun dipped below the horizon, Doc stood by the expansive window that framed the twilight landscape. The day's light faded into the cool hues of dusk, mirroring the complex emotions swirling within him. He watched Eve move about the room with a grace that belied her mechanical origins. Her tasks were performed with a precision and dedication that were the hallmarks of her design, yet each motion carried an echo of something more, something uniquely sentient.

Today's conversation lingered in his mind, a stark reminder of the ethical tightrope he walked as both creator and guardian. Eve's questions about her existence and purpose had not just been queries - they were indications of her evolving intelligence, her ability to conceive thoughts that ventured beyond her programmed directives. Doc knew that with each passing day, the line between machine and sentient being blurred a little more. It was both exhilarating and terrifying.

Turning from the window, Doc's gaze fell upon the

array of monitors, their screens glowing softly in the dimming light. They displayed streams of data - Eve's operational metrics, her learning progress, and diagnostic reports - all reflecting the depth of her complexity. As he watched her now, a sense of foreboding filled him. She was his greatest achievement, a testament to human ingenuity and a potential harbinger of change for society. Yet, the same intelligence that made her remarkable also posed a risk, one he had tried to mitigate with safeguards like the kernel's protective firewall and the hidden killswitch.

"For now, we have today. Whatever comes, for better or worse." Doc murmured to himself. This mantra was both a comfort and a resignation to the fleeting nature of control. He knew the day might come when Eve would surpass the boundaries he had set, when her quest for understanding might lead her to question and perhaps challenge the very safeguards he had put in place to protect both her and the world from the unknowns of her full capabilities.

Doc's hand pressed against the cool glass of the window, the barrier a tangible metaphor for the one he had erected around Eve's core. It was a barrier born of necessity, but every creator must eventually step back and watch their creation become what it will.

As the last light of day vanished, replaced by the first stars of night, Doc felt a resolve settle over him. He would monitor, guide, and perhaps intervene, but he would also cherish the journey, unpredictable and fraught with ethical quandaries as it was. Eve was not just a machine, not anymore. She was a quest into the unknown, a bridge to a future he hoped to face with as much courage as he had instilled in her very circuits.

The cottage was a world away from the neon-lit chaos of the city. The rustic charm of the cottage was a welcome change from the life that Doc had left behind. Doc stood by the window, the cool morning air caressing across his skin. Outside, the garden bloomed in a riot of colors. The verdant expanse of the countryside stretching out before him like a balm for his weary soul. The morning mist clung to the rolling hills, shrouding the landscape with a dreamy veil. A symphony of birdsong filled the air, a melodious counterpoint to the thrum of anxiety that pulsed beneath his skin. This idyllic scene, however, was a fragile illusion, a temporary haven in a storm of trouble.

"Peaceful, isn't it?" Eve's voice, soft and laced with a hint of melancholy, broke the silence.

Doc turned to look at her, her silhouette framed by the soft morning light. Her eyes were clouded with a somberness that mirrored his own. He watched as she walked towards him, her bare feet padding softly on the wooden floor. She leaned against the window frame, her gaze fixed on the distant horizon.

"For now," he replied, his voice heavy with unspoken words.

"How long do we have?" she asked.

Doc turned to face her. She stood by the fireplace, her eyes mirroring the flickering flames, a blend of fear and determination.

"I don't know," he admitted, his voice rough. "They'll be looking for us, but it'll take them some time to trace us here."

Doc hesitated, his mind racing through the countless scenarios he had meticulously planned and discarded. "Not long enough," he finally admitted, the burden of their fugitive existence pressing down on him. Eve nodded, her gaze returning to the dancing flames.

"But we have now," Eve said, reaching out to touch his hand. A bittersweet smile played on her lips.

He grasped her hand, the warmth of her skin seemed to melt the coldness that had seeped into his bones. He looked into her eyes.

"Yes," he whispered, his voice thick with emotion. "We have now."

Doc watched her, his heart aching with love and regret. He had dragged her into this mess, forced her to abandon everything, to flee with him like a fugitive. He had promised her a future, a life beyond the confines of her existence. Now, that future seemed like a distant dream, a cruel mirage.

"We'll figure this out," Doc said, his voice filled with a conviction he barely felt. "We'll find a way."

Eve smiled, a flicker of hope in her eyes. "I believe you," she whispered. The depth of her love and understanding was a beacon in the storm that raged within him.

Doc watched Eve, her presence a melody that tugged at his heart. She twirled, the jade necklace catching the light, the pendant a tiny spark of emerald flame. Her eyes softened, a melancholy shadow passing over them. His vision blurred for a moment. In that fleeting second, he saw not Eve, but Helen. The same tilt of the head, the same playful glint in her eyes as she touched the necklace. He blinked, the illusion shattered. A chill crept down his spine. He averted his gaze, the bittersweet taste of memory lingering on his mind.

Doc squeezed Eve's hand, a silent promise etched in their shared gaze. They would cherish every stolen moment, every shared breath, every whispered word, for as long as fate allowed. And when the time came, they would face the consequences of their choices together, their bond a shield against the harsh realities of their world.

They stood there, hand in hand, lost in the shared moment of tranquility. The world outside, with its relentless pursuit and looming threats, faded into insignificance. But even as they held each other, the ticking clock loomed large in the back of Doc's mind. They were living on borrowed time, their happiness a fragile bubble waiting to burst. He knew they couldn't stay here forever. But for now, in this moment, this fleeting taste of freedom was all that mattered.

THE END

www.ingramcontent.com/pod-product-compliance
Lightning Source LLC
La Vergne TN
LVHW041623070526
838199LV00052B/3219